Ladybird  Readers

Noisy Party

Series Editor: Sorrel Pitts
Text adapted by Hazel Geatches
Song lyrics by Wardour Studios

LADYBIRD BOOKS

UK | USA | Canada | Ireland | Australia
India | New Zealand | South Africa

Ladybird Books is part of the Penguin Random House group of companies
whose addresses can be found at global.penguinrandomhouse.com.
www.penguin.co.uk   www.puffin.co.uk   www.ladybird.co.uk

Penguin
Random House
UK

Text adapted from *Pablo and the Noisy Party* by Andrew Brenner and Sumita Majumdar,
first published by Ladybird Books Ltd, 2020
Based on the *Pablo* TV series created by Gráinne Mc Guinness
This Ladybird Readers edition published 2021
001

Text and illustrations copyright © Paper Owl Creative, 2021
Pablo copyright © Paper Owl Creative, 2015

PAPER OWL FILMS

Printed in China

A CIP catalogue record for this book is available from the British Library

ISBN: 978-0-241-47549-2

All correspondence to:
Ladybird Books
Penguin Random House Children's
One Embassy Gardens, 8 Viaduct Gardens, London SW11 7BW

MIX
Paper from
responsible sources
FSC® C018179
www.fsc.org

Noisy Party

Based on
the Pablo TV series

Picture words

Pablo

Lorna

Mum

Noa

Draff

Mouse

Wren

Llama

Tang

present

party

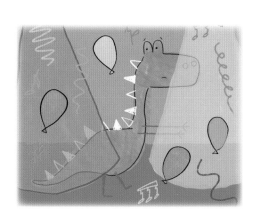

noisy

drop

necklace

It is Lorna's birthday today.

Pablo and Mum drive
to Lorna's house.

Pablo has a present.

It is purple and yellow.

Pablo likes the colors.

There is a party at
Lorna's house.

It is very noisy!

Pablo does not like the noisy party.

He drops the present.

Pablo goes back to the car.

It is not noisy in the car.

Pablo draws his friend Noa.

"What's this?" asks Noa.

"It's a party," says Pablo.
"It's very noisy."

"I don't like the noisy party!" says Noa.

Noa sits in the car with Pablo.

It is not noisy in the car.

18

Draff and Mouse are
here, too.

"What's this?" asks Mouse.

"Don't open it!" says Pablo.

"It's a party!" says Noa.

"It's too noisy!" says Mouse.

"We don't like it," says Draff.

The four friends sit in the car.

It is not noisy in the car.

More friends come.

Wren opens the present.

It is a necklace.

"The present is not
a noisy party!" says Llama.

Pablo and the friends sing
a happy song.

Lorna comes out of the house.

"Pablo doesn't like noisy parties," says Mum.

"That's OK," says Lorna.

Pablo is happy! He gives the present to Lorna.

Activities

The key below describes the skills practiced in each activity.

🖊 Spelling and writing

📖 Reading

💬 Speaking

🎧 Listening*

❓ Critical thinking

🎵 Singing*

✦ Preparation for the Cambridge Young Learners exams

*To complete these activities, listen to the audio downloads available at www.ladybirdeducation.co.uk

Match the words to the pictures.

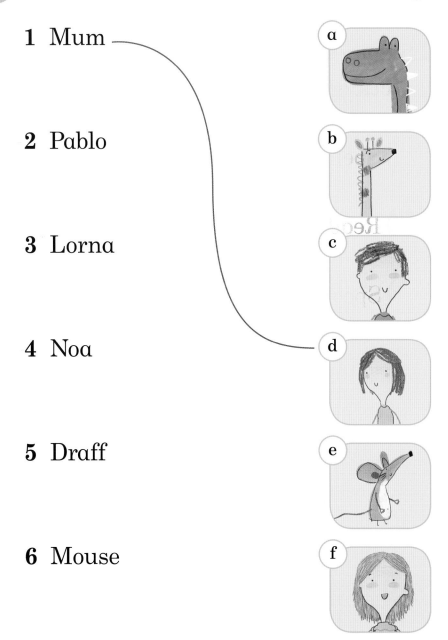

1 Mum

2 Pablo

3 Lorna

4 Noa

5 Draff

6 Mouse

a

b

c

d

e

f

2 Look and read. Put a ✓ or a ✗ in the boxes. 📖 ⭐

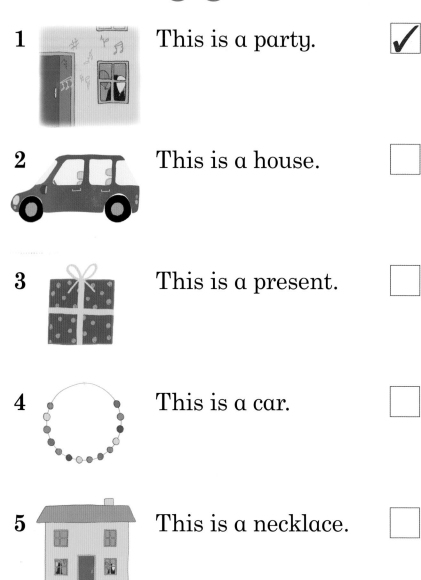

1 This is a party. ✓

2 This is a house. ☐

3 This is a present. ☐

4 This is a car. ☐

5 This is a necklace. ☐

3 **Look at the pictures. Look at the letters. Write the words.**

1 siyon

n o i s y

2 snetper

....

3 yaprt

....

4 encekcal

....

5 podr

....

4 **Circle the correct words.**

1 The present is purple and
green. / (yellow.)

2 Wren opens the **present. / purple.**

3 It is a **party. / necklace.**

5 **Circle the correct sentences.**

1  **a** The party is noisy.
b The party is not noisy.

2  **a** Pablo drops the present.
b Pablo does not drop the present.

3  **a** It is noisy in the car.
b It is not noisy in the car.

4  **a** Wren opens the present.
b Wren does not open the present.

6 Find the words.

party
present
drop
noisy

paterrsatrpartyignpresentnosdroplfnoisy

34

7 Find the words. 📖

m	o	t	r	s	o	l	b	f
n	o	i	s	y	p	s	a	t
a	e	r	l	p	a	r	t	y
d	o	p	c	k	h	r	g	o
r	n	e	c	k	l	a	c	e
o	r	d	c	i	p	l	l	y
p	n	j	a	h	o	u	s	e
c	r	s	r	b	s	t	y	m

noisy   house   car

necklace   party   drop

8 Listen and color.
Use the colors below. 🎧 🌸

9 **Ask and answer the questions with a friend.**

1
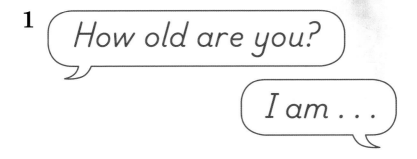

How old are you?

I am . . .

2 When is your birthday?

3 Do you like parties?

4 Do you like noisy parties?

10 **Look and read. Write *yes* or *no*.**

1 There are four animals.   *yes*

2 The boy has brown hair.

3 The car is green.

4 There are two flowers.

5 The boy is in the car.

11 **Choose the correct words and write them on the lines.** 📖 ✏️ ⭐

present   car   noisy

house   party   necklace

It is Lorna's birthday today. Pablo

has a ¹ present for Lorna. There is

a ² .... at Lorna's ³ ....

The party is very ⁴ ....

Pablo does not like the noisy party.

He goes back to the ⁵ ....

39

12 Do the crossword.

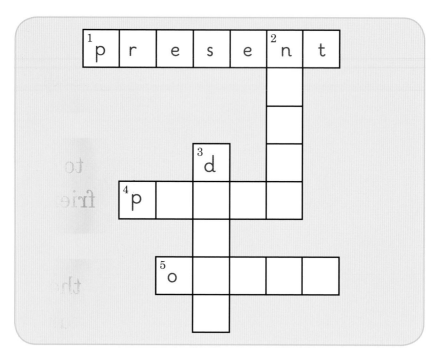

Across

1 Pablo has a . . . for Lorna.

4 Pablo does not like the . . .

5 Wren . . . the present.

Down

2 The party is . . .

3 Pablo . . . the present.

13 **Match the words.**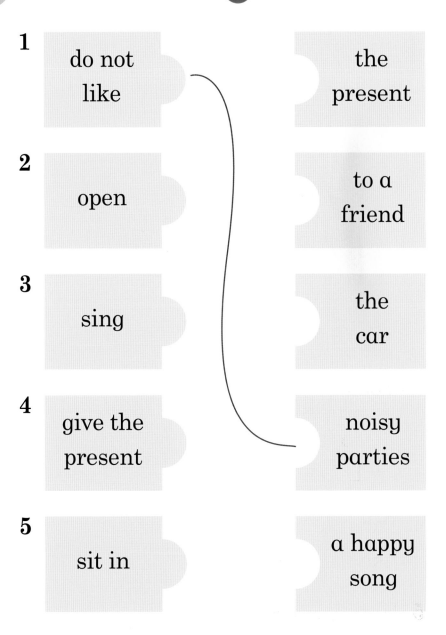

1 do not like

the present

2 open

to a friend

3 sing

the car

4 give the present

noisy parties

5 sit in

a happy song

14 **Look at the picture and read the questions. Write one-word answers.**

1 Where is Draff?

Draff is in the .... car ....

2 Is Wren in the car?

........................., he is not.

3 What is in the present?

A ....

15 Put a ✓ by the things you can see.

1	flowers	✓	**2**	animals	
3	a man		**4**	a girl	
5	trees		**6**	a necklace	
7	a car		**8**	a school	
9	a present		**10**	a cat	
11	a boy		**12**	a dog	
13	books		**14**	a house	

16 Write the missing letters.

es   is   se   ac   ar

1  p r e _s_ e n t

2 p _____ _____ t y

3  n e c k l _____ _____ e

4  h o u _____ _____

5  n o _____ _____ y

17 **Work with a friend.**
Talk about the picture.

1 What is this?

This is a present.

2 What color is it?

It is . . .

3 Is it for Mum?

Yes, / No, . . .

18 Who says this?

Mum   Noa   Lorna   Pablo

1 "Pablo doesn't like noisy parties,"

says .... Mum ....

2 "That's OK,"

says ....

3 "Don't open it!"

says ....

4 "What's this?"

asks ....

19 Sing the song.

The party is noisy.
I don't like it.
The party is noisy.
Let's sit in the car.

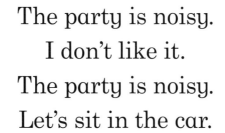
Lorna is having a party.
Lots of her friends are near.
Pablo comes, and there is music
and talking.
The car is not noisy. Let's sit here.

The party is noisy.
I don't like it.
The party is noisy.
Let's sit in the car.

All his friends are in the car.
It is very quiet in this place.
Lorna comes, and they give her a present.
Lorna loves her new necklace!

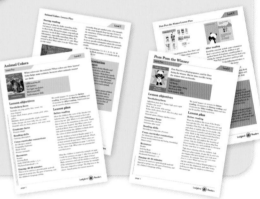